THE STORY OF
Princess Victoria

LARISSA BOUYETT

AuthorHouse™
1663 Liberty Drive
Bloomington, IN 47403
www.authorhouse.com
Phone: 1 (800) 839-8640

Published by AuthorHouse 10/15/2018

ISBN: 978-1-5462-6217-6 (sc)
ISBN: 978-1-5462-6218-3 (e)

Library of Congress Control Number: 2018911610

Print information available on the last page.

authorHOUSE®

INTRODUCTION

This is a story of a girl named Victoria from De'Victoria, Barcelona, who became a princess after meeting her prince on a cruise. Victoria's dad opened a Spanish Bakery-Restaurant in the United States. They also own a very famous Bakery-Restaurant in Barcelona named De'Victoria Reposteria y Restaurante. Phillipe is the prince of Spain, who went on a cruise with his family to explore the different islands in the Caribbean.

CHAPTER ONE

Victoria is a young lady who lives with her parents and her younger brother. Her parents own a famous bakery in Barcelona named De'Victoria Bakery that started back in the 1900s. One day Victoria's father, Ferdinand, had the idea to move to the States to open a Spanish bakery. After much research and talk with the family, they decided to move.

Ferdinand's younger brother took over the family business in Barcelona so Victoria's family could move to the States. Victoria was ten years old and her brother, Alfonso, was three years old when they moved. They grew up in a big house and went to school where they made lots of friends while their parents worked at the bakery. The bakery is a famous place where families visit and have the most delicious Spanish pastries in all Fort Lauderdale. On the weekends, the kids spend a couple hours helping their parents in the bakery.

CHAPTER TWO

It is Victoria's eighteenth birthday.

Ferdinand asked, "Victoria, what do you want to do for your birthday? It is a big one."

Victoria said, "Let's go on a cruise, Dad. I want to explore the Caribbean islands."

Ferdinand said, "Well, a cruise it is."

It was the first time the family had gone on a cruise. They got on the ship and the kids were amazed by how big and beautiful the boat was. After they unpacked, the whole family explored the ship by checking the stores, restaurants, and what shows were playing on that day and the other six days. Victoria's family went to the welcome counter and booked tours in

Key West, Puerto Rico, and St. Thomas. The first night on the ship Victoria was eating at the restaurant with her family and she noticed a handsome man sitting at the table next to her. He looked at her and said, "Good evening!" Victoria's eyes just lit up.

After dinner, Victoria went for a walk and saw the handsome man she had seen at dinner.

As he approached Victoria, he says, "Hi, my name is Phillipe."

Victoria replied, "Hi, I'm Victoria."

They smiled, and Phillipe walked off to meet his parents.

The first stop was in Key West. While Victoria and her family were at a restaurant having lunch, Prince Phillipe happened to walked by with his family and from a short distance he waves "Hi" to Victoria. He then kept walking with his parents. Victoria and her family had a great time in Key West. They stopped in the many stores on Duval Street, and, of course, they returned to the ship with lots of souvenirs from the island.

Back on the ship that evening, Victoria and Phillipe met and went for a walk until it was time for dinner. While walking, he told her who he was and where he was from. She couldn't believe she was talking to a prince! They decided to sit by the pool and talk about their families, his royal experiences, and how wonderful it was for them to meet and spend time together. They agreed to get together the next day since it was time to meet their respective families for dinner.

CHAPTER THREE

Day three was at sea. The prince knocked on Victoria's door to ask her if she wanted to have breakfast with him and his family, but her parents said no. While Victoria and her family were at the pool, Phillipe walked by and invited Victoria and Alfonso to watch the *Star Wars* show with him at 3:00. Her parents gave them permission to go with Phillipe. Since Victoria, Alfonso, and Phillipe had plans, Ferdinand and Sofia went to see a 1980's show where they happened to see Phillipe's parents across the way of the theater where they were sitting.

On day four, the ship stopped in Puerto Rico.

"What a beautiful island!" said Victoria.

The best part about stopping in Puerto Rico was that the people spoke Spanish, and Old San Juan looks very Spanish so it felt like their home away from home. While walking, they stopped in a store where Victoria saw a beautiful blue and purple bracelet. Ferdinand could see how his daughter loved the bracelet, and since it was her favorite colors, he wanted to buy it for her as a memory from Puerto Rico. Somehow, the prince found out that she had bought the beautiful bracelet. Knowing that soon they would be separated, he bought her a charm with two red hearts as a symbol of their time together and to always remember him by. After enjoying a day in Puerto Rico, and its Spanish food, it was time to go back to the ship.

The fifth day was at sea. It was another day at the pool and watching shows that were scheduled for that day. At one point when Victoria and her family were at the pool overlooking the ocean, they spotted a family of dolphins swimming next to the ship. It was so beautiful! Later that day, Phillipe and Victoria met again and had snacks on the boardwalk.

On the sixth day the ship stopped in St. Thomas. The whole family went to the beach and on the way back, before returning to the ship, they stopped to shop at the different kiosks. Once they were back on the ship, everyone was so tired that they decided to go to dinner and just relax.

Soon it was "Captain's Night" and everyone had to dress up. Victoria wore a beautiful purple and blue dress with sparkling white stones all over it. Prince Phillipe looked stunning in his black suit with a light blue shirt. It just happened that both families were to be seated at the same time. So, they decided to sit together. They talked about their time on the ship, their different tours they booked on the islands, and they shared their stories about their lives in Spain.

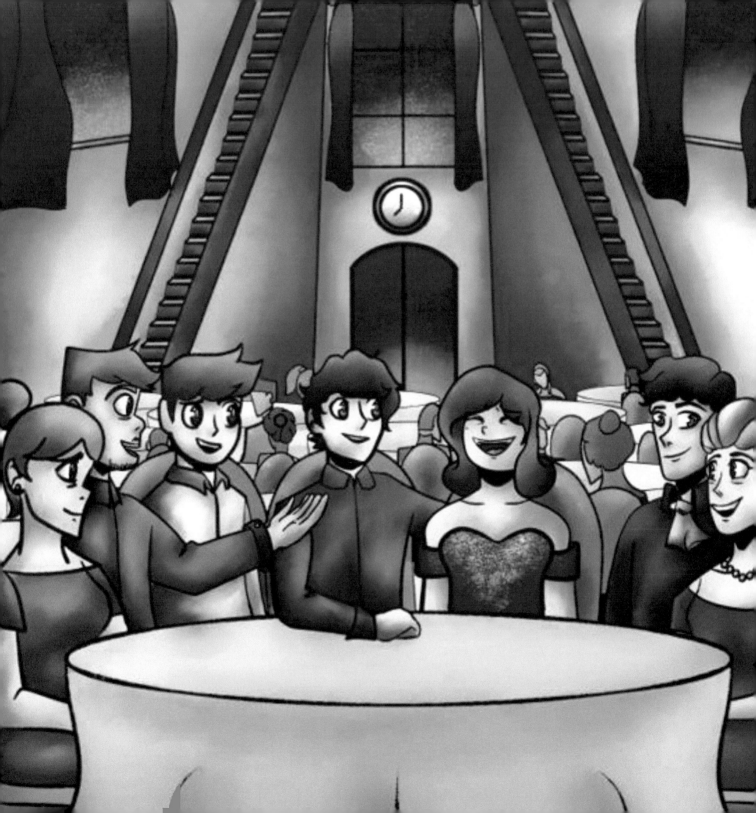

The cruise was coming to an end. Day seven, which was the last night on the ship, it was a sad day for Prince Phillipe and Victoria since they were not going to see each other again. They asked their parents if they could keep in contact. "Of course!" they said to them. So, they shared phone numbers and hoped that one day, when Victoria returned to Barcelona, they could see each other again.

It was time to leave, and Phillipe could see Victoria's watery eyes while he was saying good-bye to her.

CHAPTER FOUR

One day while Victoria was home reading a book, Prince Phillipe called her. What a wonderful surprise! Victoria was so happy to hear from him. They talked for hours about Victoria's experience at the university, their families, their adventures, and future plans.

After a year of talking on the phone, they finally decided to see each other again. Prince Phillipe invited Victoria to visit him in Spain so they could spend some time together and see if their love for each other was still strong.

Of course, it was! When Victoria landed at the airport and they saw each other, it was like the first day they met on the cruise. The prince took her around Asturias, see to the beautiful mountains, and religious sites. He showed her where he was born and how the people of Spain loved him as a prince for how he treated them and always looked after their needs.

Prince Phillipe bought a beautiful and unique sparkling ring while visiting Puerto Rico, thinking that one day he would give it to Victoria. Before he asked her to visit him in Spain, he asked her family for her hand in marriage. At the palace the cooks prepared a fabulous special Spanish traditional dinner Asturiana, a rich stew made with Asturian large white beans, pork shoulder, morcilla, chorizo, and saffron. After the family gathered together at the table, the prince went to get Victoria in her room. What she didn't know was that the prince flew in her family to celebrate their engagement.

"Victoria," Phillipe said, "it is time to go and have dinner. Everyone is waiting."

Victoria opened the door wearing a stunningly beautiful dress. Her hair was styled with long curls.

When she opened the door, she saw the handsome man with whom she fell in love with. It was like a fairy tale. Victoria told him how handsome he looked, and he replied, "You look gorgeous."

While holding hands, Phillipe and Victoria walked through the palace toward the dining room where Victoria saw her whole family. She said, "My family is here. What are they doing here?"

The prince told her, "I invited them for a special dinner. Once we are done with dinner, we are all going to the Royal Room."

That was where Prince Phillipe was going to propose.

At dinner, Victoria told her family what they had done that day, and the many places Phillipe had taken her. At one point Victoria even mentioned to her parents that she was considering moving back to Barcelona, but before she made that decision, she wanted her parents to give their approval.

Prince Phillipe, being the comical self that he was, started making jokes trying to change the subject and, of course, everyone at the table followed his lead. Victoria was upset because her parents ignored her.

"Victoria," the prince asked, "what is wrong?"

"Well, I was ignored by my family when I asked such an important question. Everyone changed the subject." Victoria replied.

Prince Phillipe says to Victoria, "Come on, Victoria, don't get upset about that, I'm sure that they will agree. We can talk about it after dinner when we all meet in the Royal Room."

He kissed her on the forehead, and she fell for his line.

Throughout dinner, there were jokes between the families and stories about when they were growing up. Ferdinand talked about how he moved his family to the States and opened his own business, but his dream is to return to their hometown in Barcelona.

The royal family said to everyone, "It is time to go to the Royal Room where we can sit comfortably and get to know each other more."

Once they were all seated, the prince got on one knee and asked Victoria,

"Will you marry me, Victoria? I would like for you to live with me until we grow old, have kids together, and be happy forever."

Victoria was amazed, but before she could say yes, she looked to her parents for approval.

The prince told her, "Victoria, they know. I already asked for your hand, and they are here to support me and give their approval."

She looked at him and said, "If that is why they are here, then yes, I accept."

Phillipe's dog, Rocky, brought the ring to him, and when he opened the case, she couldn't believe how beautiful the ring was.

CHAPTER FIVE

Alicia, the daughter of the royal family's maid who had been with the royal family for years, grew up with Phillipe and liked him since she was a teenager. When she found out about Victoria, Alicia was jealous that Phillipe wanted to marry Victoria. She wanted to make it impossible for them to be happy.

Every night Alicia would look at the prince and wink and throw kisses to him in front of Victoria, but Victoria was so sure about his love for her that she didn't pay any attention to Alicia. One night while Victoria was on her balcony, Alicia came in the room to bring her some green tea. She approached Victoria and told her, "I'm sorry, Victoria, but I think you should know about the prince and me."

Victoria said, "Okay, tell me your story, and so you know, I will confront him about it."

"No problem," Alicia said. "I'm sure he will deny everything."

Alicia went on to tell her, "Before you came into the picture, we had feelings for each other. But because I'm the daughter of a maid, his parents didn't accept the relationship. That is why they went on a cruise: to take him out of his environment and away from me. My parents had to take me to my grandmother's house in France where I lived for a year. That is why he started talking to you, because I wasn't around."

Victoria asked Alicia, "So how come you are back? Who approved for you to come back?"

Alicia told her, "Because my grandmother passed, and I had no place to go. I had to come back. What you don't understand is that the royal family loves my family. We've worked for them for years, so they felt obligated to take me back."

Victoria said, "Well, this is something that I will have to talk to Phillipe about. Also, if he didn't love me, he wouldn't have given me the ring and asked me to marry him."

The next morning, Prince Phillipe knocked on Victoria's door, and when she opened it, he had her favorite breakfast: eggs with toasted bread and green tea.

After they had breakfast on the balcony, Victoria told him about the conversation she had with Alicia the night before. Phillipe hung his head in shame. Victoria asked, "Is it all true, what she said? Answer me, honestly."

Prince Phillipe told her, "It's not all true. The relationship between Alicia and me is somewhat true, but I was not in love with her. She was in love with me and still is. Look, Victoria, I'm not going to lie to you. We did have something together, but it was nothing like you and I have. I want to marry you because of who you are as a person. We are perfect for each other. If she is a bother, we can get rid of her."

Prince Phillipe then told Victoria, "Alicia is getting married in a couple of months to someone she met at school."

Victoria felt better after she spoke with Phillipe about what Alicia had told her the night before and she was able to enjoy the remainder of her day with her future husband.

CHAPTER SIX

The wedding preparations started and Victoria's family decided to move back to Barcelona. Returning to Barcelona would make it easier to prepare for the wedding of their beautiful daughter. It would also allow her to be close to the prince. The wedding was to take place in March so they only had eight months to prepare.

Victoria trusted that the prince was telling her the truth, but one day while she was at the royal family's house, she noticed that the prince was talking to Alicia in the kitchen, so she hid behind the wall to listen. The prince told Alicia, "I love Victoria and don't want anything to come between us. If you do something to jeopardize that, I will make sure that you don't work here anymore."

Alicia responded, "Don't worry, I'm getting married in a couple days to the man I love, but I will never forget what we had when we were younger."

Phillipe said, "Alicia, that is in the past."

Alicia was very hurt by his comment. Meanwhile, Victoria ran to the other room so they would not see she was listening. Alicia happened to walk to that room and saw Victoria. They said hello to one another, and Alicia then walked away.

Before Alicia's wedding, Victoria approached her and asked, "Is everything okay? I noticed you are avoiding me lately."

Alicia replied back saying, "Everything is fine."

When Victoria turned around, Alicia told her, "Stop! No, everything is not okay. I know Phillipe told you that he has no feelings for me, but I know he does!"

Alicia then left the room.

The royal family attended Alicia's wedding out of obligation; Prince Phillipe attended with his fiancée at his side. When Alicia threw the bouquet, she made sure that Victoria didn't catch it.

CHAPTER SEVEN

A month before the wedding, a good friend of Alicia's knocked on Victoria's door and gave her an envelope.

Victoria asked, "Who are you?"

But Alicia's friend just walked away and never answered. In the envelope was a letter that Phillipe wrote to Alicia right before she left to live with her grandmother. In it, he told Alicia how he felt about her and how he was going to missed her. Victoria showed the letter to Phillipe, he had nothing to say other than that he agreed to what happened between them. The prince told Victoria how much he loved her and that he no longer had feelings for Alicia. Their relationship had happened many years before. He asked her to please forget about it and to move on with the wedding. Victoria didn't forget, so she started her own investigation with the other maids. One of them told Victoria everything because she never liked Alicia or her family. She described how Alicia's family abused the royal family by lying to them about things they did behind their back.

After talking to different people Victoria realized it was in the past and with Alicia married, Victoria and Phillipe could live happily together. Victoria decided to follow her heart and continued preparing for her day.

Finally, the wedding day arrived. Victoria looked beautiful in an off-white wedding dress with a long tail of crystals designed just for her. Prince Phillipe waited anxiously for her at the altar, his sparkling eyes looking at his future wife. Victoria was so happy to see Prince Phillipe wearing an elegant blue suit waiting for her at the altar.

Over the years Prince Phillipe and Princess Victoria travelled the world representing Spain with high honor. They had three beautiful children, Emilio, twin girls, Rose and Juliana.

They lived happily ever after

Printed in the United States
By Bookmasters